ZOG
and the
FLYING DOCTORS

By Julia Donaldson

Illustrated by Axel Scheffler

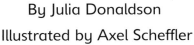

ALISON
GREEN
BOOKS

Meet the Flying Doctors – a dragon, knight and girl.
Their names are Gadabout the Great,
and Zog, and Princess Pearl.

Pearl gives people medicine
and pills and vaccinations,

And Gadabout is expert
at performing operations.

Zog is good at flying, though not quite so good at landing,
But Gadabout and Princess Pearl are always understanding.

Flying high one morning they heard a mermaid wail.

"I'm sunburnt and it hurts!" she cried, and swished her scaly tail.

Bang-crash-thump they landed.

The mermaid's skin was red.

Pearl rubbed in some
special cream.
"And wear this hat,"
she said.

"Thank you!" said the
mermaid, and she
waved a fond goodbye
As the team of flying
doctors sped away
into the sky.

As the sun rose higher they saw a unicorn.

He pawed the ground and whinnied, "I've grown an extra horn!"

Bang-crash-thump they landed. "I'll help you," said the knight
And he cut the horn off gently, to the unicorn's delight.

"Thank you," said the unicorn,
        "for taking so much care,"
And the team of flying doctors
        sped away into the air.

Halfway through the afternoon
they heard a lion sneeze.
"I've caught the flu," the lion roared.
"Can someone help me, please?"

Bang-crash-thump they landed,
and Pearl said, "Take this pill.
And do keep warm!
That's terribly important when you're ill."

But the lion's cave was chilly,
    so Zog said, "Fetch some wood."
Then he breathed out lots of flames
    until the fire burned bright and good.

As evening fell, they saw a great big palace down below.

"My uncle's house!" said Princess Pearl. "Let's go and say hello."

Bang-crash-thump they landed.

Pearl's uncle was the king.

He didn't say hello. Instead he said,

"You naughty thing!

"Where *have* you been?" he thundered.

"You look an awful mess.

What's happened to your crown?

And where's your pretty, frilly dress?"

"But, Uncle, can't you see that I'm a

doctor now?" said Pearl.

The king replied, "Princesses can't be

doctors, silly girl!"

He told his men to seize her and to lock her up inside.
Princess Pearl was furious. She stamped and stormed and cried.

Weeks went by, and Princess Pearl spent many weary hours
Sewing pretty cushions and arranging pretty flowers.

The others tried to rescue her
    with all their might and main,
But they simply couldn't manage –
    all their efforts were in vain.

Each night they flew to visit her
and perched upon her sill,
And one dark night she told them
that the king had fallen ill.

The king grew worse: his head was sore,
his arms and legs felt weak,
His skin had turned bright orange
and he found it hard to speak.

He called a lot of doctors –
    a new one every day.
He croaked, "What is this illness?"
    but they simply couldn't say.

They didn't know the answer,
but Pearl was pretty sure.
"It looks like orange fever,"
and she read about the cure:

"Grated horn of unicorn,
a mighty lion's sneeze,
Some mermaid's scales, a little
slime, and half a pound of cheese."

She told the others what to get.
  "And do be very quick!
My uncle could be dying –
  he looks extremely sick."

Away flew Zog and Gadabout.
  They reached the lion's den.
Bang-crash-thump they landed.
  He sneezed for them, and then . . .

They flew back to the forest,
  where the grateful unicorn
Was very pleased to give them
  his unwanted sawn-off horn.

Back to the mermaid's rock they flew.
She gladly gave some scales,
And her sea-snail friends allowed
them to collect their slimy trails.

Zog said, "I'm exhausted!"

but he flew and flew, until . . .

Bang-crash-thump he landed
on the bedroom windowsill.

Princess Pearl said thank you
for the scales, the slime, the sneeze,
And the horn (which then she grated up
with half a pound of cheese.)

She tiptoed to her uncle's room.
The king lay in his bed.
She held a spoonful to his mouth.
"Now, open wide," she said.

After just one spoonful
    her uncle felt much stronger,
And after spoonful two
    he wasn't orange any longer.

After spoonful three, the king
    was dancing with delight.
"Princesses *can* be doctors –
    you were absolutely right!
I'm sorry that I locked you up.
    Of course you must go free,
But do come back to
    visit me – and bring
        your friends to tea."

"Hooray!" cried Pearl, and out she ran
to join the other two.

Then off into the sunset sped the flying doctor crew.

For Jez and Filiz – J.D.

For Alice, Maxime and Dimitri – A.S.

First published in the UK in 2016 by
Alison Green Books
An imprint of Scholastic Children's Books
Euston House, 24 Eversholt Street
London NW1 1DB, UK
A division of Scholastic Ltd
www.scholastic.co.uk
London – New York – Toronto – Sydney – Auckland
Mexico City – New Delhi – Hong Kong
This Early Reader edition published 2014

ISBN: 978 1 407189 54 3